Here
Comes
Herb's
Hurricane!

Here Comes Herb's Hurricane!

by James Stevenson

Harper & Row, Publishers
New York, Evanston, San Francisco, London

Library of Congress Catalog Card Number: 73–7138
Trade Standard Book Number: 06–025782–2
Harpercrest Standard Book Number: 06–025783–0

FIRST EDITION

TO
G.N.H. & O.M.

Chapter
1

"This is probably the most perfect day I've ever seen in my entire life!" cried Herb, the plump brown rabbit, striding down through the meadow in the warm sunlight, his long ears flapping. It was a clear morning in September, and Herb's young nephews, Harvey and Pete, were trotting along behind him, trying to keep up. "Look at the sea!" exclaimed Herb, pointing toward the beach. "Look at the sky!" He waved toward some wispy clouds, floating high overhead. "Have you *ever* seen a day like this?" he asked.

"I haven't," said Harvey.

"Me, either," said Pete.

"Feel the breeze!" exclaimed Herb. "Observe the wildflowers, bending this way and that!"

"It's a nice-looking day, Uncle Herb," said Harvey, "but is anything going to happen?"

"Such as what?" asked Herb.

"Oh, I don't know," said Harvey. "Something exciting or interesting."

"I believe it will," said Herb.

"Good," said Pete.

"What do you think it will be?" asked Harvey.

"Well, I don't know," said Herb, sniffing the air. "Too soon to say. Something extraordinary, no doubt. Say, I believe I smell grapes."

"Grapes?" said Pete. "Oh, boy."

"Where?" said Harvey.

Herb glanced over at the woods. "Smells as if there might be a few grapes over there, boys," he said.

"We'll take a look," said Pete.

"See you later, Uncle Herb," said Harvey. The two nephews raced across the field toward the woods.

Herb climbed over the old stone wall, and walked along the dirt road that ran along the shore. He had gone only a few steps when he saw Clyde, a very old turtle with a flaky shell, crawling toward him.

"Good day, Clyde!" Herb exclaimed. "How are you, sir?"

Clyde turned his head gradually, and peered up at Herb with a wet-looking eye. "Oh, it's you, Herb," he said. "What are you doing? Walking about, I suppose?"

"Exactly," said Herb. "It's a glorious day, isn't it?"

"Oh, I don't know about that," said Clyde. "It's just another day as far as I'm concerned. I'm crawling along as best I can—getting no-where, and more slowly every day."

"You look well, Clyde."

"That's just appearances, Herb. One thing

about turtles is, we start out looking old and awful, and then—when we finally do get old and awful—you can't tell the difference. But *I* can tell. Every part of me is tired."

"That's too bad," said Herb. "Why don't you rest a bit? Sit in the shade awhile?"

"Oh, I've tried that, believe me," said Clyde. "It's a bore. I'd rather crawl around and get exhausted. Maybe I'll go down to the club for a bit."

"Well, it's a grand day for a walk."

"September days can fool you, Herb. They start out sweet and pretty, and by nightfall you've got yourself a hurricane."

"A hurricane?" repeated Herb.

"Trees falling over, branches snapping, wind howling, devastation across the land," said Clyde. "Yes, indeed."

"Not today, I'd bet," said Herb.

"Don't count on it," said Clyde. "I remember a day very much like this about sixty years ago. Maybe seventy. I can't remember dates, or anything else either. Maybe it was twenty years ago...." Clyde paused. "It couldn't have been *last* year, could it?" He shook his head. "No. It wasn't last year. Well, whenever it was, it started with a peachy day like this, and everybody was frolicking around, enjoying the sunshine. By noon, the sky was kind of yellowy-green, and the wind started doing funny things. It was eerie. Then it began to howl, and pretty soon the waves were coming right over the beach and into the marsh. All night long it stormed, and everybody thought it was the end of the world. They crouched down in their holes and houses, scared to death...." Clyde's voice faded away, and he blinked slowly several times.

Herb waited impatiently, then finally asked, "What happened next, Clyde?"

"What happened when?" answered Clyde.

"During the hurricane," said Herb.

"What hurricane?" asked Clyde.

"The one you were just telling me about," said Herb.

"Oh," said Clyde, "*that* hurricane...I don't

remember. Well, maybe I do. I don't remember if I remember. Wait a minute." Herb waited. Then Clyde started again. "Oh, yes," he said. "It was frightful. I got rolled up into the woods, end over end, by a great gust of wind. My shell was crashing into rocks and trees, banging about—oh my!"

"It must have been a dreadful experience," said Herb.

"The noise was awful," said Clyde. "Next morning, it was a beautiful day again, but everything was in a different place. The entire beach was smooth sand where there used to be rocks. Oh, you never can tell what will happen come September, Herb. It's the hurricane season, and I strongly recommend that everybody stay inside their shell."

"That's good advice, Clyde," said Herb. "Well, I'll see you." He waved and started down the road again.

"Don't count on it," called Clyde. "I'm on my last legs."

"You look spry to me," said Herb.

"Oh, I may have a few years left," said Clyde. "On the other hand, I may not."

"Just keep out of the way of hurricanes," called Herb cheerfully. "So long."

Clyde crawled toward the shade of a clump of yellow ragweed. "Hurricanes?" he murmured. "Hurricanes? Why did he say that? There hasn't been a hurricane around here as long as I can remember...."

Herb strolled on down the dirt road, thinking about what Clyde had told him. Suddenly, a large gray rabbit came charging around a curve in the road, and almost crashed into Herb. It was Graham, Herb's cranky cousin, jogging.

"Watch where you're going!" yelled Graham. "Oh, it's only *you....*" Graham stopped, gasping and panting. "Do you have to walk in...the middle...of the...road?" he demanded, between gasps.

"Sorry, Graham," said Herb. "Just enjoying the day. What are you doing?"

"I'm building my strength," said Graham, his chest heaving. "Staying in shape...getting in trim....*Some* rabbits take a little pride in their appearance, you know." Graham stared at Herb. "Why don't *you* jog?"

"Oh, I don't know," said Herb. "You miss a lot if you move too fast."

"Well, I haven't time to dilly-dally and dawdle," said Graham. "I have important things to do. Pardon me." He pushed past Herb, and went trotting down the road—his ears straight up, his elbows pumping—and vanished. A cloud of dust floated upward in the sunlight, and drifted away.

Herb walked on. A gentle wind, salty and wet, came in from the sea. The leaves on the trees fluttered lightly, and high overhead a sea gull swooped across the sky. "Hurricanes," thought Herb. "We ought to be prepared for hurricanes."

A shadow sailed across the road, just ahead of Herb. "Good morning, good morning, good morning!" shrilled a piercing voice. Herb looked up, and saw Cyrus, the sea gull.

"Oh, hello, Cyrus," said Herb.

"Hi, Herb," said Cyrus, making a fast turn, and landing on the road. "Did you happen to notice me upstairs just now, when I was soaring? Did you see those big, graceful turns I was making? How'd I look? Did the sunlight sort of catch my wings? Did I kind of gleam and glisten? What was your impression?"

"I didn't actually pay too much attention, frankly," said Herb. "I was thinking about something else."

"Well, I felt I was particularly stunning," said Cyrus. "I don't want to sound boastful, but I've been practicing a lot, and I think I'm getting more beautiful every day."

"Everybody is entitled to their own opinion," said Herb.

"I hope you don't think I'm a show-off," continued Cyrus. "The fact is, I'm hoping to catch the eye of a nifty little gull named Marsha—lives out on one of the rocky islands. I've got a terrible crush on her. I think I'm in love."

"I'm very happy for you," said Herb. "Tell me, Cyrus, what's the weather going to do? I notice the sea looks rather quiet."

"Quiet?" repeated Cyrus.

"Yes," said Herb. "Does that mean anything?"

"I don't believe so," said Cyrus, peering at the sea over his long beak. "It's just a nice day is all."

"Things could change, I suppose," said Herb. He squinted at the horizon. "Things could change...."

"You mean, a storm?" asked Cyrus.

"I don't want to alarm anybody," said Herb.

"You don't alarm me," said Cyrus, looking

nervous. "Tell me quick—is there a chance of a storm?"

"A storm," said Herb, "is always a possibility. A storm, or a hurricane...."

"A *hurricane*!" shrieked Cyrus, trembling. "Is there going to be a *hurricane*?"

"Let me put it this way," said Herb. "This time of year, there's always a chance. Maybe just one in a million, but...a chance."

"What can we do about it?" asked Cyrus. "You're the leader around here, Herb. You tell."

"We can all do our part," said Herb.

"Yes, I'm for that," said Cyrus. "Oh, my goodness, a hurricane."

"We can remain calm," continued Herb. "We can take precautions, and be prepared."

"Oh, good!" said Cyrus. "I'm so glad you're always in charge, Herb. What can *I* do? Anything special?"

"Let me think a minute," said Herb. "What are you good at?"

"Flying, I guess," said Cyrus. "I'm good at flying."

"Well, how about being a look-out? How about flying way up and far out to sea, and giving the warning if there are any signs of a storm coming?"

"I could handle that," said Cyrus. "Sure."

"I'd assign somebody here on land to watch you, to see if you give the warning signal."

"What's the warning signal?" asked Cyrus.

"Well," said Herb, "how about flying three loop-the-loops?"

"Three loop-the-loops?" repeated Cyrus. "No problem."

"Excellent, first-rate, and splendid," said Herb, rubbing his paws together. "Now we've got ourselves a warning system, just in case."

Cyrus said, "We're really lucky to have you in charge, Herb. I don't know what would happen if we didn't have a leader." Herb nodded in agreement. "But one thing," continued Cyrus. "I was just wondering—is there going to be some sort of title for my job?"

"What do you mean?" asked Herb.

"An official title," said Cyrus. "Some people think I'm sort of silly, you know? I get excited about things and I fly around a good deal, and some people laugh at me. If I had an official title, it would make my job a lot easier."

"Hmmm," said Herb. "I don't see why not. How about 'Look-Out'?"

Cyrus shrugged.

"How about 'Official Look-Out'?" asked Herb.

"It's OK, I guess," said Cyrus.

"Well, what about 'Chief Look-Out'?"

"That's better...."

"Perhaps 'Aerial Observer'?" suggested Herb.

"Now you're talking," said Cyrus, nodding.

Herb paused for a moment, then said, "'Commanding Sea Gull in Charge of Operation Skywatch'!"

"Wow!" exclaimed Cyrus. "Perfect! I'll take it!"

"Good," said Herb.

"I'll go on duty right now," said Cyrus, getting ready to take off. "What's that warning signal again?"

"Three loop-the-loops," said Herb.

"Aye, aye, sir," screeched Cyrus, and flapped away into the sky.

Herb watched him go, then resumed his walk down the road. Herb was beginning to feel that things were getting organized. "We're off to a good start," he said aloud, and began to walk more briskly down the road.

Chapter **2**

As Herb walked along the road, he could hear the Kipneys, Rudy and Blanche, chattering in the woods just ahead. Mr. and Mrs. Kipney, the squirrels, lived in a large maple tree, and they were always very busy. They had cleared away all the plants and bushes and shrubs and grass from around their maple tree, and Rudy Kipney had made a sidewalk of flat stones leading all the way from the road to their front door. Now he was adding a border of seashells to the sidewalk.

"Hello, Rudy!" called Herb, as he approached.

"Oh, greetings, Herb!" called Rudy, glancing up from his work. "How do you like our new sidewalk? Kind of tones up the place, don't you think?"

"Very handsome," said Herb.

"Everybody should have a sidewalk," said Rudy. "When I finish this, I'm going to make a terrace in back, and some nice little walls, and maybe a pool with a place to sit."

"You have a lot of work ahead of you," said Herb.

"The hard part was getting the whole place cleared out—chopping down trees, digging up shrubs, that kind of thing—but now it's beginning to look the way we want it. After I finish the pool and the place to sit, I think I'll make a path around the woods back there. Maybe have a border of seashells along the edges. Then I think maybe I'll put in a few benches along the path so people can sit down and look at the scenery. I think that would be nice. I'll plant a few trees here and there, and put in a fountain. Maybe put some ferns and stuff around the fountain. Then you'd really have something to look at. I wonder if it would be a good idea to have a statue on the fountain? A little art, you know? Maybe I could get Dunlop the beaver to carve something nice. Do you think he's any good?"

"I don't know," said Herb. "Probably."

"He's a proud, unpleasant sort of creature, I know that. I wonder if he'd do what I want —a good-looking statue of a squirrel standing on a branch, something handsome and inspiring like that. Or would he carve some weird thing everybody would hate?"

"I guess you'd have to talk to him," said Herb.

"I haven't got the time to fool around right now," said Rudy. "The day isn't long enough for what I have to do." He bent down and added more seashells to the sidewalk.

Blanche Kipney called from across the dirt yard. "Are you coming to our party tonight, Herb?" She was stirring something in a large pot. "We're having twenty or thirty animals."

"I certainly plan to," said Herb. "Thank you." He paused for a moment. "Are you at all worried about the weather?"

"Weather?" said Rudy. "You mean rain?"

"If it rains," said Blanche, "we'll just move everybody under the tree."

Herb said, "There's been some talk about a storm, maybe even a hurricane."

"Hurricane!" exclaimed Rudy. "Oh, come on, Herb. That's utter nonsense!"

"Well," said Herb, "this time of year you never can tell. It's always a possibility."

"Rubbish!" said Rudy. "Not a chance!"

"I just want everybody to be warned."

"You're a wild one, Herb," said Rudy, chuckling. He clapped Herb on the back good-naturedly. "Heh, heh, heh."

Herb's ears began to get red; he felt insulted. "All right, Rudy," he said. "Just remember I warned you."

"Come here, Herb," called Blanche. "I want you to try this dip I'm making for the party." Herb walked over, and Blanche scooped some mushy stuff out of the big bowl onto a skunk-cabbage leaf, and rolled it up. "It's a mushroom-acorn mix," she said, handing it to him.

Herb took a bite. "Oh, that's delicious," he said. He finished it off. "Just delicious."

"We're having a lot of other things, including, of course, carrot sticks," she said.

"Carrot sticks," said Herb. "Splendid."

Blanche went back to stirring the dip in the bowl, and Herb said goodbye, and walked back to the road.

"See you tonight, Herb," called Rudy. "Unless there's a hurricane!" He winked. Herb did not reply. When Herb was out of sight, Rudy said to Blanche, "Isn't that just like Herb? Worrying everybody about a hurricane?"

"Typical," said Blanche.

"He just wants to be in charge of everything," said Rudy. "If there isn't anything to be in charge of, he'll make it up." He put down several seashells, and stepped back to admire his work.

Herb was already fifty yards down the road, murmuring to himself. "They don't seem to respect my opinion a great deal," he mumbled. He was thinking so hard about his own hurt feelings that he almost stepped on Stanley, the garter snake, who was sunning himself in the warm dirt in the middle of the road. "Ooops!" said Herb. "Sorry, Stan. Didn't see you."

Stanley raised his head an inch or so. "Oh, that's perfectly all right," he said. "Nobody ever seems to notice me. I'm used to it. Just step all over me."

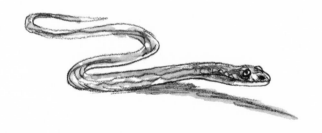

"I apologize, Stan," said Herb. "Frankly, I was thinking about something else."

"No need to apologize, Herb. I'm the bottom rung around here socially. All day long I'm ignored. Everybody tromps around with their noses in the air, nearly squashing me with their big feet. One of these days, I'll get flattened for keeps, and then my worries will be over. Not that anyone would notice, or care that I'm gone." Stanley sniffed softly.

"Oh, come on now, Stan," said Herb. "Everybody likes you a lot."

"I'm not complaining, Herb," said Stanley. "I don't complain. I understand very well that everybody has more important things to think about than not stepping on me. I keep my feelings to myself. I'm not a whiner."

"You're very good about it, Stan."

"I *could* make a fuss, but I don't. I just go my way."

"You have a wonderful attitude," said Herb.

"Nobody will ever know how much I suffer," said Stanley. "Are you going to the Kipneys' party tonight?"

"Why, yes," said Herb. "Are you?"

"Certainly not," said Stanley. "I can't stand parties. I've been trying to keep out of sight, so they wouldn't invite me."

"Well, maybe you should get out of the road, Stan," said Herb. "They might spot you out here."

"You think so?" asked Stanley. "I guess you're right. I was just catching a bit of sun, but now that you mention it, I better slither off into the grass, out of sight. I wouldn't want to hurt their feelings by telling them I wouldn't come to their dreadful party. I'm very considerate of people's feelings."

"I know you are," said Herb, starting to walk down the road again. Stanley followed him.

"I wonder," said Stanley, "what the Kipneys are going to try to force on everybody in the way of refreshments at their dreadful party."

"Well, Blanche is making a mushroom-acorn dip, and some other things," said Herb.

"Mushroom-acorn dip," repeated Stanley. He was silent for a moment. Then he said,

"Well, they certainly are getting la-di-da, aren't they? Not my kind of party, not by a long shot. What else are they having?"

"I don't know," said Herb. "See you later, Stan." He began walking.

"I suppose so," said Stan. "Unless I get stepped on. I think I'll soak up a little more of this sunshine, then I'll be wiggling away. So long, Herb." He settled down once more in the middle of the road, and closed his eyes.

A bit farther along the shore was Graham's house, and since Herb did not particularly want to bump into Graham jogging again, he turned into the woods and took a short-cut back toward his own house in the meadow, climbing over old, forgotten stone walls and following narrow, winding paths that had been worn smooth years and years ago, but now were overgrown—blocked in places by fallen branches, vanishing under thick clumps of ferns, interrupted by tall saplings. But Herb knew his way, and presently—pushing aside a heavy tangle of vines—he was back in his own

meadow, striding toward his house in the sunlight.

"Hey, Uncle Herb!" called Harvey. He and Pete were standing by Herb's white picket fence, eating grapes.

"Hello, boys," called Herb. "What's up?"

"We found the grapevine," said Pete, munching. "We brought some for you." He held up a bunch.

"Thank you, Pete," said Herb. He swung open the gate. "Come on in."

Herb led the way through his small yard and garden, and into the front door of his house. The house—one large, comfortable room dug out of the side of the meadow—was cool and dim, with an excellent view of the sea from the doorway. Herb sat down in an old, torn beach chair, ate a grape, and gazed out at the water. "Mmm...wonderful," he remarked. "Perfect," he added.

"The grapes?" asked Pete.

"The grapes, the view, the day, the company —everything," said Herb.

Harvey and Pete went inside to examine some shelves at the back of the room. The shelves were piled with things that Herb had found, at one time or another, along the beach. There were stones and shells of every size and texture and color; pale-pink crab claws, orangey-brown seaweed, sticks as smooth and shiny as ivory, bits of deep-green glass, rusty nails, frayed ropes, wooden signs with the words worn off, light-green grasses, fish

hooks, twine, broken branches, cinnamon-colored beer cans, a torn map, and a padlock that had rusted shut. "You sure have got a lot of junk here, Uncle Herb," said Harvey.

"*Junk?*" said Herb.

"Well, not junk, exactly," said Harvey quickly.

"More like *stuff*," said Pete. "You have a wonderful collection of stuff."

"Why, thank you," said Herb. "There's more in that big box in the corner. Mostly items I haven't had time to sort out as yet." Harvey and Pete immediately peered into the big box, and began poking around with a great clatter. Pete lifted out a broken telescope, and Harvey found a red-and-white-striped lobster-pot buoy.

"Tell me, boys," said Herb, after the noise subsided, "would you be able to make a long rope out of vines?"

"Sure," said Harvey.

"What kind of vines?" asked Pete.

"That would be up to you," said Herb. "It would have to be strong, though. Maybe honeysuckle, or wisteria, or bittersweet. Maybe some of each.''

"How long a rope?" asked Harvey.

"Well," said Herb, "do you know that waterfall in the woods where Kirkham the frog lives?"

"Of course," said Harvey.

"It should be long enough to go from Kirkham's waterfall all the way across the meadow to my house right here."

"Wow," said Pete.

"We can do it," said Harvey.

"Excellent," said Herb.

"What's it for?" asked Pete.

Herb looked at his nephews thoughtfully for several moments.

"Is it a secret?" asked Harvey.

"We can keep secrets," said Pete. "We know plenty of things we've never told. Plenty."

"Tell us," said Harvey.

Herb still did not reply.

"If you can't tell us *that* secret," said Pete, "will you tell us some other secret?"

"Any secret," added Harvey.

"Well, it's not exactly a secret," said Herb finally. "I just don't want to get the whole community stirred up. I want to do this right."

Harvey and Pete nodded. Herb gazed out to sea some more. Then he said, "I have heard from a highly-placed reliable source that there is a chance of a possible hurricane."

Harvey's and Pete's eyes popped, and Pete dropped his grapes on the floor. "Wow," said Harvey. "A possible hurricane!"

"Now," continued Herb, "I feel that it is my duty to make sure that everybody around here is protected."

"You're sort of the boss, aren't you, Uncle Herb?" asked Harvey. "You're usually in charge of things."

"Oh, I wouldn't say that exactly," said Herb, shifting his beach chair slightly. "But people do seem to turn to me for leadership. I don't know why...." He folded his paws modestly, and gazed at the floor.

"It's because you're the one everybody respects," said Harvey. "You're smart, and you know what to do."

"You think so?" said Herb. He had been brooding about how Rudy Kipney had laughed at him. "That's your opinion?" asked Herb.

"Yop," said Harvey.

"Mine, too," said Pete, gathering up his grapes, and wiping off the dirt.

"I'm glad to hear that," said Herb. "Sometimes I'm not too sure. I like almost everybody, and I'm awfully pleased when they like me."

"About the vine and the hurricane," said Harvey. "You were saying...."

"Oh, yes," said Herb. "There may be a hurricane, and there may not. But we must be prepared. We must take care of our friends."

"Yes, we must," said Harvey.

"But how?" asked Pete.

"My plan is to organize an alarm system, a warning, so that everybody could take shelter in case of a storm—I've got to make sure that everybody is safe."

"That's a wonderful idea, Uncle Herb," said Harvey.

"Everybody would be really grateful," said Pete.

"Let's get started then," said Herb, standing up. "There's work to be done!"

"Come on, Pete," cried Harvey. "We've got to get going on that vine!"

"Right!" cried Pete, and the two young rabbits dashed out of the house. A moment later, Harvey reappeared in the doorway.

"Oh, Uncle Herb?" he said. "I forgot to ask. What's the vine for?"

"It's a vital, important, and essential part of the warning alarm system," said Herb. "I'll show you what it's for when you're finished."

"OK," cried Harvey, and ran away once more.

Herb rubbed his paws together, and walked over to the big box in the corner. He peered into the dimness, and poked about until—with a loud, pleased "Ha!"—he found what he was looking for.

Chapter
3

Herb climbed down from his roof, and looked up at what he had just done. The bell, a rusty old bell he had found in the box in the corner, was now hanging from the branch of a birch tree, just above the roof. Herb had tied it loosely with a length of bittersweet vine. "Excellent," murmured Herb. Then he turned and marched toward the woods in search of Desmond, the squirrel, who lived by the stream.

Desmond was swinging from a branch high up in an elm tree, near his nest of sticks and leaves.

"Oh, Desmond," called Herb. "Could I bother you for a moment?"

Desmond looked down. "Hello, Herb!" he called. "Just doing a few exercises. I'll be right down!" He did a somersault, landed on the branch below, jumped to the one below that, caught it with his front paws, swung up and over, did a back-flip, and landed lightly on the ground next to Herb. "I feel great!" he said. "It's all a matter of staying in shape, you know?"

"I believe you're right, Desmond," said Herb.

"A squirrel that can't jump from branch to branch is no better than a rabbit—" Desmond stopped abruptly. "Oops. Sorry, Herb. I didn't mean anything personal. It's just a saying we have among squirrels. Heh, heh." Desmond looked very embarrassed.

"I understand," said Herb.

"It doesn't mean that rabbits aren't first-rate in every way, you understand," continued Desmond. "It's simply that they can't jump around very well in trees. You get it?"

"Sure, Desmond. Don't give it a thought. It's just a saying."

"Exactly, Herb. It shouldn't hurt your feelings."

"It doesn't," said Herb. "Heavens, rabbits have sayings about squirrels, too. It's the same idea."

"They do?" said Desmond. "Like what, for instance?"

"Oh, it doesn't matter. Just sayings."

"I'm just curious," said Desmond. "It doesn't make any difference to me. Heh, heh. What do they say?"

"You really want to know?"

"Certainly," said Desmond. "Why not?"

"Well, you might get upset."

"*Me?*" said Desmond. "Are you kidding?"

"Well, let's see," said Herb. "Oh, we say—"
He started to laugh.

"What's so funny?" demanded Desmond.

"Nothing," said Herb, trying not to laugh.

"Let's hear it," said Desmond. "Come on.
You can't hurt *my* feelings."

"Oh, all right," said Herb. "There's one saying among rabbits that goes like this.... Uh,
well, what they say is—you know, if somebody
is acting sort of, well, uh—the saying is, I believe, 'Calm down—you're acting like a squirrel.'" Herb cleared his throat, and gazed at the
sky. There was a long silence.

Finally, Desmond spoke in a whisper. "Rabbits say *that*?" he asked. "About *us*?"

"Not very often," said Herb quickly. "Rarely—very rarely."

"I just can't believe it," said Desmond, after a while.

"I personally never say anything like that about squirrels, Desmond," said Herb. "I have nothing but admiration for the way they climb and jump and everything. You squirrels are amazing."

"I feel the same way about rabbits," said Desmond. "The speed with which they move along the ground...."

"I admire squirrels' agility and strength," said Herb.

"What impresses me about rabbits is their calm, thoughtful intelligence," said Desmond. "Wisdom, I guess you'd call it."

There was another silence, and then Herb spoke. "I wanted to ask you a favor, Desmond," he said. "On behalf of the community."

"Sure," said Desmond. "What?"

"Well, there seems to be a chance of a hurricane coming," Herb began. He explained the danger, and Desmond listened carefully, nodding from time to time. "My plan is to organize a warning system," Herb finished, "and I thought maybe you'd like to help."

"Naturally," said Desmond. "What do I do?"

"Well," said Herb, "Cyrus the sea gull has volunteered to be look-out. He's going to fly way out to sea and watch for any signs of a big storm coming. If he sees any, he's going to fly three loop-the-loops."

"Three loop-the-loops, eh? As a signal to us?"

"Exactly," said Herb.

"And my job?" asked Desmond.

"I thought you might be in charge of looking out at the look-out. You'd stay up in your tree and watch Cyrus to see if he does three loop-the-loops."

"I can do it!" exclaimed Desmond. "I'm steady and I'm calm and I'm dependable! You can count on me!" He ran up the side of the elm tree.

"Wait!" cried Herb. "I'm not quite finished."

Desmond ran back down again. "I'm listening, Herb. Don't think I'm not listening. I'm giving you my full attention, and you can count on me!"

"I just wanted to tell you what to do if you see the signal from Cyrus."

"Of course, of course!" said Desmond. "What do I do?"

Herb stepped over to a sunflower that stood on the bank of the stream. "My idea," said Herb, "is that you take a sunflower up in the tree with you—" He broke off a large bloom. "My, doesn't that look splendid?" he said. He handed the flower to Desmond. "You take that up in the tree with you—" he continued.

"I take this up in the tree," said Desmond. "Got it so far."

"—and if you see Cyrus doing his loop-the-loops, you drop the sunflower out of the tree and down into the stream."

"I drop it down into the stream," said Desmond.

"Well, that's *your* part of it, Desmond," said Herb.

"That's all?" said Desmond. "Just drop the sunflower in the stream? That's too easy."

"I'm glad you're confident," said Herb. "Then nothing will go wrong."

"You can count on me," said Desmond. "What happens to the sunflower?"

"It floats down the stream toward the waterfall," said Herb.

"Yes, and then?"

"It goes over the waterfall."

"Then?"

"That starts Part Two of the warning system."

"It does?" said Desmond. "Wow. What happens?"

"No time to explain right now," said Herb. "I've got to keep moving. There are instructions to be given, plans to be made, orders to be issued."

"Shall I get started with my sunflower?" asked Desmond.

"Immediately," said Herb.

Desmond stuck the sunflower in his teeth, raced up the side of the tree, and vanished among the leafy branches. A moment later he called down, "I'm all set, Herb!"

"First-rate, excellent, and splendid!" called Herb. "Keep your eye on Cyrus!" Herb started walking away along the bank of the stream, heading for the waterfall and Kirkham's place.

As he walked, Herb greeted the animals that lived near the stream: Alfred, the chipmunk; Earl and Irene, the snails; Gus, the slug; and a number of birds who happened to be in the neighborhood. He mentioned the possibility of a hurricane to each one, hurriedly, and said that there would be an alarm system set up so that they would have time to take shelter. Irene the snail looked very frightened. "What's the alarm?" she asked.

"You'll hear a bell ringing," said Herb. "That will be the signal to run for shelter."

"I *can't* run," said Irene. "What will I do?"

"Move as rapidly as possible," said Herb. "There will be ample time, due to the warning system. Remain calm."

"Oh, I'm so glad you're in charge, Herb," said Irene.

"We're all grateful, Herb," said Earl, inching away toward a dry hollow on the side of the stream. "Follow me, Irene," he said. "Let's pick a good shelter ahead of time."

The birds said that they would pass the word around the community, and Herb continued on his way toward the waterfall feeling very good; things were certainly getting organized.

Kirkham was not at home. Herb looked under a large log for the old frog, but Kirkham was not there so Herb sat down on a mossy rock at the edge of the pool. He watched the waterfall, and listened to the sounds of the water as it tumbled and gurgled down the hillside. It was nice to rest for a moment, Herb

thought. Kirkham could not be far away; Kirkham rarely traveled. The waterfall made all kinds of music as it rushed around the rocks, over small dams and twigs and grasses and leaves, through narrow places, splashing down into broad pools with bubbles floating on the dark surface; there were marvelous roarings and garglings and tinklings and gulpings, and, in the midst of it all, Herb thought he heard Kirkham's deep bass voice singing, but he couldn't see him anywhere. Herb watched an oak leaf travel down the stream, turning this way and that, spinning through the rapids, then diving over the falls, vanishing in the foam below, then reappearing and drifting across the quiet, shallow pool near Herb's feet. "If I had to live someplace other than in the meadow," thought Herb, "this is where I'd like to live."

He heard the singing again, and suddenly Kirkham, green and wet and shiny, came out from behind the waterfall, blinking his enormous eyes. "Why, hellooo, Herb," he boomed,

"I was just taking a shower." He crouched down, then jumped over to Herb's rock in a single, enormous leap, landing with a great splat, spraying water in all directions.

"How are you, Kirkham?" asked Herb.

"What?" said Kirkham. "I can't hear you."

"HOW ARE YOU?" yelled Herb.

"Let's get away from the waterfall," said Kirkham. He leaped up the bank, and Herb followed. "I can never hear anybody around my waterfall," said Kirkham. "Nobody else seems to have a big voice like mine, or they all mumble. I don't know which, and I don't care either. If I wanted to hear every dumb thing every person says, well, I wouldn't live by the waterfall, would I?"

"I guess not," said Herb.

"Well, what's up?" asked Kirkham. "Any big news outside of the woods, over in the meadow, down at the beach?"

"Not really," said Herb.

"Didn't think so," said Kirkham.

"I wanted to ask you a favor, Kirkham," said Herb.

"As long as it doesn't involve my leaving the immediate area," said Kirkham. "I'm not enthusiastic about travel."

"No, you wouldn't have to leave," said Herb. "You could handle the whole favor right from your own waterfall."

"It sounds pretty good so far."

"All you have to do is watch the waterfall."

"That's what I do anyway," said Kirkham.

"I know," said Herb. "That's why I picked you for the job. Now here's the other part of the favor. We're going to get a long vine strung from my house all the way across the meadow and into the woods to your waterfall. Now if you see a sunflower come over the waterfall, you pull the vine."

"Wait a minute, wait a minute," said Kirkham. "This is suddenly getting very complicated. I'm not ready for all this. A vine is coming over the waterfall, I pull some sunflower—"

"No, no, Kirkham," interrupted Herb. "A sunflower may come over the waterfall, and if it does, you pull the vine. That will make a bell ring over at my place—"

"This is too much," said Kirkham, blinking rapidly. "I'm getting nervous. I mean, there I was taking a nice shower, then all of a sudden I'm all mixed up with sunflowers and bells ringing and vines. Maybe you should get yourself another frog, Herb."

"I'm sorry, Kirkham. I didn't mean to upset you. I realize this is very sudden—"

"Darn right it is," boomed Kirkham.

"—but it may be an emergency," said Herb. "In case we have a hurricane."

"A hurricane?" repeated Kirkham.

"Just a chance," said Herb, "but we do want to be prepared. You're part of the alarm system, so people can take shelter."

"Why didn't you say so in the first place?" thundered Kirkham. "I'm perfectly willing to do my share. Just explain it one more time. And a little slowly. Especially the part about the sunflower."

"Certainly," said Herb, and, as Kirkham gazed at him, blinking from time to time, Herb went through it once again.

Chapter
4

Arthur Malloy, the portly woodchuck, had slept late. He came out of his house in the woods, smelled the grapes and honeysuckle that twisted on their vines around his porch, listened to the bees humming, and gave a great yawn. "Oh, my," he said, feeling the warm sun on his fur, "this is all right." He stepped to the edge of his porch, and sat down heavily. "Yes, indeed," he said, leaning against the railing, and letting his eyes half close. The grape leaves provided a bit of shade, but plenty of sunlight came through. A mild breeze made the honeysuckle tremble. Arthur folded his paws across his broad paunch, and let his eyes shut entirely.

"Arthur?" It was the voice of Mrs. Malloy, from the kitchen. "Are you busy?"

"What?" said Arthur, opening his eyes, and getting quickly to his feet.

"Are you very busy?" called Mrs. Malloy.

"No, my dear," called Arthur. "Not very busy. I'm...sort of medium busy."

"Well, I have a list of things that must be done immediately. If you're not too busy."

"Perhaps I can find time to fit in a few," said Arthur. "Although I do have rather a full schedule."

Mrs. Malloy came out onto the porch, and handed Arthur a large piece of paper with a great deal of writing on it. "These are the really important things to be done," she said. "After you finish these, I have another list."

"Hmmm," said Arthur, peering at the list. "Yes," he mumbled. "I certainly must get these things done.... Just a matter of planning... organizing my time...."

"Do the errands first. If you hurry, you'll be back in time to do the raking and the clipping and the weeding before lunch, and you can do the other list in the afternoon."

"That's exactly the way I intend to do it," said Arthur. He folded the list carefully. "I'd better get started right away."

Arthur stepped off the porch onto the woods path, and waddled away, holding the list tightly. The sunshine lay in small, uneven pools on the path, coming down through the trees; there were bright places, and dark places where the shadows seemed to float, and when the breeze moved the tree tops high above, the blobs of light and shade on the path drifted this way and that. Arthur's house was out of sight now, and Arthur began to walk a little more slowly. He yawned a couple of times, and paused to smell some honeysuckle. "Ahhh," he murmured. "You can't beat honeysuckle." Perhaps he'd sit down for just a moment, enjoy the honeysuckle—but then he remembered his list of things to do. He gazed at his list, but the words seemed to run together. "Lettuce," he said aloud, and continued walking down the path. "Two heads of lettuce...."

Under the tallest tree in the woods, where Edgar, the owl, slept in the daytime, the path divided. One part went along the stream, down past the waterfall, toward the shore; the other part went toward the club. The club? "No, sir," said Arthur to himself. "No time to waste sitting around the club today. Too many things to do. Can't lose a minute. It would be out of

the question this morning to go to the club
…where it's cool…and dark…and very
pleasant…very pleasant indeed." He stood
still for a moment. "Even if sitting in the old
club for a moment *would* give me a bit of rest
…help me gather my strength so I could do all
these errands.…Why, if I were to go to the
club for a minute or two, I might feel very
much refreshed. Renewed. Full of energy.
Then I'd dash through all these errands, and
go trotting back home, and get the next list,
and do even more things!" Arthur considered
this carefully, then stepped over the stream,
and took the path toward the club, walking
much faster.

The clubhouse was old, and surrounded by
tall weeds and shrubs. Shingles were sticking
up from the roof where wisteria vines had
worked their way under them; honeysuckle
had climbed the walls. Paint was peeling
off the doorway, and several windows were
broken; gray cobwebs filled the empty spaces.
Arthur pushed open the creaky front door, and

peered into the dark room. "Hello," he said. "Anybody here?" He could just make out the vague shapes of the old pool table, the sofa, the wicker chairs. The light coming through the dusty windows made the room gold in some places, dim in others. It was very quiet and cool.

Something moved on the pool table. "Who's that?" asked Arthur.

"Who's *that*?" replied a sleepy voice.

"It's me—Arthur."

"Well, it's me—Clyde." The old turtle was lying on the pool table. "I was just catching forty winks. How are you, Arthur?"

"Fine, Clyde. But awfully busy today."

"You want to use the pool table?" asked Clyde. "I'll get out of your way."

"No, no, Clyde. You stay put. I'm too busy. Got a million things to do."

"You sure? I can sleep anywhere, you know. Anywhere and anytime. It's the staying awake I find difficult...I like to nap on this pool table because it feels good."

"I'm only here for a second, between er-rands," said Arthur. "Look at the list of things I have to do today." He showed Clyde his list. Clyde peered at it.

"Say, you *are* busy," said Clyde.

"That's why I thought I'd come in for a moment and take a break," said Arthur, sitting down with a sigh in one of the wicker chairs. It creaked and groaned.

"Very sensible," said Clyde, drowsily. Then he was asleep again.

Arthur leaned back in his chair. "Oh, I do like this place," he said to himself. "It's just ...nice." His eyes began to close, and soon he was snoring gently. His paw fell open, and the list slid out, drifting lazily down through the dusty sunlight toward the dim dirt floor. It landed without any sound at all.

Half an hour later, Earl the snail was inching along the top of the meadow, keeping a sharp eye out for changes in the weather, when he heard Graham, the grouchy gray rabbit, hailing him. "Earl!" cried Graham. "Oh, Earl!"

Earl turned his head, and saw Graham jogging through the tall grass toward him. "Good morning, Graham," he said. "How are you?"

"I'm looking for a game of Acorn," said Graham. "Want to play?"

"I'm not much on sports," said Earl. "Besides, aren't you worried about the hurricane?"

"What hurricane?" asked Graham.

"Herb said there might be a hurricane," said Earl.

"Hurricane!" roared Graham. "There's no chance in the world of a hurricane. That's a typical nutty idea of Herb's. He just wants an excuse to run around and tell everybody what to do."

"Oh," said Earl.

"He just wants to act important," said Graham. "Now, how about a quick game of Acorn?"

"How do you play? Do you have to run much?"

"No," said Graham. "There's no running at all. Come on." He led Earl onto a flat spot at the top of the field. "It requires two acorns," he explained. "You have an acorn. I have an acorn. We place our respective acorns on the ground here, side by side. You follow me?"

"So far," said Earl.

"Very well," said Graham. "Now, you see

that big apple tree at the bottom of the meadow?" He pointed down the hill. "That's the goal."

"The goal?" repeated Earl.

"Right," said Graham. "The idea of the game is to see who can get their acorn to hit that apple tree first. The first one to hit the tree wins."

"How do you do that?" asked Earl. "It's a long way off."

"You usually throw it or kick it," said Graham, quickly placing two acorns side by side on the ground. "I personally prefer to kick it."

"Hmmm," said Earl. "I'm not too good at kicking. As a matter of fact, I'm not too good at throwing, either."

"Don't worry!" cried Graham, doing some practice kicks. "Use any method you like."

"I think I'll use the pushing method," said Earl. "That's my best method."

"Ready?" said Graham. He crouched behind his acorn, paws clenched, scowling in-

tently toward the apple tree. "On your mark
...get set...go!" he yelled. He gave his acorn
a tremendous kick, and it soared over the
meadow, falling directly toward the tree. It

missed by a few feet, and landed in the tall
grass. "Lot of wind today," cried Graham, gal-
loping away down the slope toward his acorn.

Earl was still inching toward his own acorn,

getting ready to give it a push with his nose. When he got close enough at last, he gave it a nudge. The acorn did not move. Earl backed up, and tried again. He gave it a harder nudge. The acorn wobbled a bit, but did not roll. Earl sighed. He did not want to give up, but the game was turning out to be a lot harder than he'd expected. "I'll just have to try harder," he thought. Using every bit of his strength, Earl gave one final shove—and the acorn began to roll down the hill. Earl lost his balance in the effort, and began rolling downhill after it. He went bouncing along, going faster and faster, until he crashed into a clump of thistles halfway down the slope, and came to a stop. He felt rather dizzy, so he decided to rest for a moment.

Graham, meanwhile, was at the bottom of the meadow, thrashing about in the tall grass, looking for his acorn. He couldn't find it. He kicked at the weeds and the wildflowers, grumbling. Twenty yards behind him, Earl's acorn was rolling down the hill merrily, going this way and that, bumping along toward the apple tree. Graham stopped hunting for a moment, and wiped his face, panting. It was hot, and he was extremely cross about not finding his acorn. Suddenly, behind him, he heard a soft *click*. It sounded like...like an acorn hitting an apple tree. Graham whirled around. There, nestling against the trunk of the old tree, was Earl's acorn, where it had rolled to a stop.

"I don't believe it," said Graham quietly. Then louder, he said, "It's not likely." Then he began to shout. "It's impossible!" he yelled. "Utterly *im*possible!"

"What's the matter, Graham?" called Earl, from halfway up the hill. "Can't you find your acorn?"

"No!" shouted Graham. He was furious. "I can't find my acorn, and anyway, you won. Your acorn hit the tree!"

"What?" called Earl. "I can't hear you."

"You won! You won! You won!" yelled Graham. "Can you hear *that*?"

"Who won?" called Earl, from within the thistle patch.

"Never mind!" roared Graham.

About ten minutes later, Earl arrived down at the apple tree, and saw his acorn resting against the trunk. He was very surprised and pleased. "Is this really my acorn?" he asked.

"Yes, it's your acorn," snapped Graham, still thrashing about in the tall grass. "You won."

"You haven't found yours yet?" asked Earl.

"Mind your own business," replied Graham.

Earl tried to cheer Graham up. "You were absolutely right, Graham," he said. "This is a wonderful game. Let's play again!"

"Again?" growled Graham. "Certainly not! I haven't got time to fool around with games all day."

"Want me to help you look for your acorn?" asked Earl.

"No!" yelled Graham. "In fact, I don't want to find it at all. I'm much too busy for this nonsense!" He marched away through the tall grass, and was soon headed down the road, grumbling, toward home.

Earl crept over to the apple tree, and gave his acorn a practice poke with his nose.

"Hey, Earl," said a voice overhead. "What are you doing?"

Earl looked up, and saw Eileen, the squirrel, and her little brother, Lew, sitting on one of the branches.

"Oh, hello, children," said Earl. "I'm practicing a game called Acorn."

"Oh," said Lew. "Is it hard?"

"It takes a certain amount of skill," said Earl. "But not too much. Want to play?"

Chapter 5

"You fellows did a splendid job," said Herb to his nephews, tying one end of the long vine to the short vine that hung down from the branch of the birch tree. He gave the vine a very gentle tug, and it made the bell give one soft *ding*. "Works like a charm," said Herb.

"Why don't we give it a real ringing?" asked Harvey.

"Just to make sure it works," added Pete.

"We better not," said Herb. "It would frighten everybody."

"Well, it's a first-class alarm system," said Harvey.

"It sure is," said Pete.

Herb and Harvey and Pete had just examined the vine all the way from the waterfall to the house, making sure it was strong, and strung properly through the trees, and high

enough in the branches so that nobody would set off the alarm accidentally, by tripping over it. They had fixed it so that Kirkham could reach it conveniently at his waterfall, and now that Herb had tied the other end to the bell, the whole alarm system was all set. "How about a carrot for everybody?" asked Herb.

"Sounds good," said Harvey.

"I'd like that," said Pete.

"We ought to invite the squirrel children who helped us string the vine through the trees," said Harvey. "May we do that, Uncle Herb?"

"By all means," said Herb.

"We'll go get them," said Harvey, and he ran back toward the woods with Pete.

"I'll round up the carrots," called Herb, and he went into his house. He was feeling very much like a leader. "I feel a lot better," he thought, "knowing that we're prepared for the worst."

Cyrus the sea gull flew over the rocky islands, looking for Marsha. He wanted to tell her about his important new job, and about how everybody was counting on him to warn them with his special three-loop-the-loop signal if a hurricane was coming. He hoped she would be impressed.

He spotted her standing on a high part of one of the islands. A large sea gull Cyrus didn't know was next to her. Cyrus glanced around the sky once more—no signs of trouble. It wouldn't matter if he glided down for just a minute.

He made a neat landing on the island, ruffled his feathers, and called, "Hello, Marsha!"

"Oh, hi, Cyrus," said Marsha. "How are you?"

"Very busy," said Cyrus. "I've got an important new—"

Marsha interrupted him. "This is Ronald, from down the shore," she said. "Ronald, this is Cyrus."

"Hi, there," said Ronald, hardly looking at Cyrus.

"How do you do?" said Cyrus. "Say, Marsha,

did you hear about my new—"

"Excuse me, Cyrus," said Marsha. "Ronald was just showing me his mussel-drop. It's so fantastic. Do it again, Ron, so Cyrus can see. Watch this, Cyrus. Ron's wonderful."

Cyrus tried to look pleasant. "What is it?" he said.

"The way this works, Cy," said Ronald, "is you take your mussel, or your clam, or whatever's on your menu, and fly up with it to approximately one hundred feet. Then you fly with it straight down, and you don't let go of your mussel until the last minute. Pow!"

"What was wrong with the old way?" asked Cyrus. "Just fly up and drop it?"

Ronald chuckled. "It's OK for old-timers, and sea gulls that can't fly too well. But with *my* method, you get real accuracy, and you don't get your dinner scattered all over the place." He paused. "It's a bit tricky and dangerous, however. I'd suggest you stick to the old method."

"Thanks for the advice," said Cyrus glumly.

"Listen, Marsha, I just got this big important—"

Marsha wasn't listening. "Do it one more time, Ron," she said. "Just for me?"

"No problem," said Ronald. He picked up a mussel, and flew high into the sky with it. With a whistling noise, Ronald came down toward them. At the last moment, he veered off, dropping the mussel, and the shell burst open right at Marsha's feet.

"Beautiful, Ron!" she called. "Beautiful!"

"He's wasting a lot of mussels, isn't he?" said Cyrus.

Ron came in for a landing. "Listen, Marsha, I've got to flap off," he said. "I promised a bunch of old gulls down the shore I'd put on a little show of clam-opening for them. I hate to leave, but they're counting on me."

"Come back soon, Ron," said Marsha.

"Will do, Marsha," said Ron, and he flew away.

"Isn't he wonderful?" said Marsha.

"If you can't open your own clams and mussels, I guess he's OK," said Cyrus.

"What's the matter with *you?*" asked Marsha. "Why are you so cross?"

"I'm not cross," snapped Cyrus. "I'm just in a hurry. I've got a very, very important new job, and I don't have time to stand around and watch some show-off try to drop shells on my head."

"Ron isn't a show-off," said Marsha. "He's just a very talented flier."

"Are you kidding?" said Cyrus. "I can do that stuff, but I'm too busy. With my responsibilities."

"Like what?" asked Marsha.

"Oh, you wouldn't be interested, Marsha. Besides, it's sort of secret."

"Tell me," said Marsha.

"I shouldn't even be here now," said Cyrus, scanning the sky. "I'm supposed to be working. I'll see you later, Marsha." He gave his wings a quick flap.

"Wait, Cyrus!" cried Marsha. "I'm really interested. What's your job?"

"You'll tell Ronald probably," said Cyrus.

"No, I won't," said Marsha. "He's just a casual friend."

"Are you sure?" asked Cyrus.

"Of course," said Marsha. "Tell me the secret part." She moved closer to him.

Cyrus moved closer to Marsha. "I'm Commanding Sea Gull in Charge of Operation Skywatch," he whispered.

"You *are?*" whispered Marsha.

"Yes," said Cyrus.

"What is it?" asked Marsha.

Cyrus lowered his voice even more. "It's the warning system for the entire community, in case there's a hurricane." He glanced around. "I'm the one who warns them."

"What a responsibility," murmured Marsha. "Can you do it?"

"I think so," said Cyrus.

"What do you have to do?"

"Basically," said Cyrus, "I watch the sky. If I see a hurricane coming, I give the signal, and everybody can run for shelter."

"What's the signal?"

"Three loop-the-loops," said Cyrus. "It's a lot harder than dropping clams and mussels," he added.

"Can you *do* three loop-the-loops?" asked Marsha.

"Certainly, I can," said Cyrus. "Watch—I'll show you." He took off, flying low across the water, dipping this way and that, knowing that Marsha was watching. Then he zoomed dramatically up into the sky, banking gracefully, and began his first loop-the-loop.

Chapter
6

Desmond, reclining comfortably high up in the elm tree, whistling, and waving the sunflower, and peering from time to time out to sea, saw Cyrus fly up from the rocky island and begin doing a loop-the-loop. Desmond couldn't believe what he was seeing. But then —when Cyrus did a second loop-the-loop, and then a third—Desmond ran down the tree, shrieking "Hurricane! Hurricane!" and threw the sunflower into the stream. The flower floated away downstream, toward the waterfall. Desmond jumped up and down on the bank, shouting, "Hurricane coming! Everybody run!"

Animals came darting out of their burrows and nests and holes and houses, chittering and squealing, bumping into each other. "Where?"

"What?" "When?" they cried. Edgar the owl, who slept in the daytime, was wakened by the tumult below, and, stamping out of the hole in his tree, shouted, "Some of us are trying to sleep!"

"It's a hurricane, Edgar!" yelled Desmond, from down below. "Take shelter! Run! Hide! Quick—it's a hurricane!"

Edgar glared at the clear blue sky. There weren't even any clouds, and the sun was shining. "Who says it's a hurricane?" asked Edgar.

"Herb says!" cried Desmond.

"Rubbish, Herb is an idiot!" yelled Edgar, and marched back into the nest in the tree trunk. He pushed some leaves up against the entrance to shut out the noise, and tried to go back to sleep.

Kirkham the frog, squatting close to the noisy waterfall, did not hear the animals running and shouting. He was listening instead to the sounds of the water. His eyes were half-closed, and he was feeling quite content. The sun had dried his lumpy green back, and he

was considering whether or not to catch a quick nap when suddenly the sunflower appeared at the top of the waterfall. As Kirkham watched, the flower seemed to hang on the very brink for just an instant, then plunged over the falls. Kirkham blinked. Was that really the sunflower? he wondered. The alarm? The hurricane warning? So *soon*? He must be mistaken. But there it was, spinning away in the current, and down the stream. Kirkham's eyes popped wide. "That was *it*!" he boomed. "That was the sunflower!" He jumped in the air and grabbed the end of the vine that was dangling over his head. He clutched it tightly, and began to swing back and forth, sailing out over the pool and back to the mossy rocks, and out again. In a moment, he could hear the bell, even above the sound of the waterfall, ringing wildly in the meadow.

A few minutes earlier, Herb had been sitting in his beach chair by the door of his house, thinking about how grateful everybody would be if his hurricane-warning system helped save the community from disaster. He could imagine Rudy Kipney, for example, saying he was sorry that he had laughed at Herb; he could see Rudy deciding to put up a statue of Herb in their clearing in the woods, and having a big party in his honor. He could picture all the animals clapping and cheering, and he could hear himself giving a very nice speech. Not too long, just right. He would, of course, give a lot of credit to those who had helped him; he would thank Cyrus, and Desmond, and Kirkham. And Harvey and Pete, too. "Sharing the credit is one of my good qualities," Herb admitted to himself. "I'm not stingy about that.... Another of my good qualities is the way I can organize things. Who else would have thought of my sea gull-squirrel-sunflower-frog-bell alarm system?"

At that instant, the bell above his roof began to ring. "Darn it!" exclaimed Herb. "I told Harvey and Pete not to fool with that bell!" He got up, and hurried outside, as the bell rang on and on. "Cut it out!" yelled Herb—

"Stop!" He looked around and saw Harvey and Pete coming up the meadow from the beach. *They* weren't ringing the bell. He glanced at the sky—it was still clear and sunny, so it couldn't be the hurricane. But the bell continued to ring.

Herb started to climb up on his roof to untie the bell, but before he could get very far a mob of squirrels, rabbits, skunks, chipmunks, and other small animals came running and shouting down the hill, over his roof, around his house, through his flower garden, knocked down his fence, and raced on through the field toward the road. "Hurricane!" they screamed. "Here it comes!"

Herb watched them go, then turned around just in time to get knocked flat by a very large woodchuck. "Sorry," said the woodchuck, as he lumbered through the garden. "Don't you know there's a hurricane coming? Don't you hear the alarm?"

"Of course I hear it!" shouted Herb, trying to get back on his feet. "It's my alarm!" he

cried, but the woodchuck was already gone. "And it's my hurricane, too!" Herb yelled.

Harvey and Pete climbed over the broken fence, and looked at Herb standing in his garden. "Are you all right, Uncle Herb?" asked Harvey.

"No," said Herb.

"Did something go wrong with the alarm?" asked Harvey.

"It certainly did," Herb said.

It took Herb a couple of hours to find out what had gone wrong. Kirkham blamed it on the sunflower, and Desmond blamed it on Cyrus, and Cyrus blamed it on some sea gull named Ronald.

Herb told them all to be extra careful from now on, and Cyrus flew back to the rocky island, Desmond climbed back up the elm tree, and Kirkham settled down again by the waterfall. Then Herb went around apologizing to all the animals he could find. "You have my promise that this won't happen again," he said, "unless there's a real hurricane."

Most of the animals were pretty nice about it, but when Herb got back to his house he saw that there was a group of three animals standing by his garden: Graham, the cranky rabbit; Edgar the owl; and Pam, the skunk. They all looked extremely cross.

"Well, hello there," said Herb, trying to sound cheerful. "This is a nice surprise."

"We've had enough surprises for one day," snapped Graham, glaring at him.

"We're here on business," said Edgar.

"You've upset everybody," said Pam. "The whole community is very disturbed."

"I'm very sorry," said Herb. "Would you all like to come in and have a carrot?"

"We've lost enough time today," said Graham.

"And enough sleep," added Edgar. "Dreadful hullabaloo." He made a squinty face, trying not to yawn, but it didn't help. He gave a tremendous yawn, then his beak snapped shut.

"We're a committee representing all the

animals," said Pam, "and it is our decision that
you take down that stupid alarm system immediately."

"Well, I don't know about that," said Herb.
"I just wouldn't feel right leaving the whole
place unprotected."

"The committee insists upon it," growled
Graham.

"Tell me," said Herb. "Who appointed this
committee? Or were you elected? Or what?"

"The committee was selected, picked, appointed, and elected by leaders of the community," said Pam.

"Who?" asked Herb.

"I was appointed by Pam," said Edgar.

"I was appointed by Edgar," said Pam.

"And together, by secret ballot, we elected Graham," added Edgar.

"Naturally, I was named chairman," said Graham.

"So you all picked each other?" asked Herb.

"It saved a great deal of time and fuss," said Pam.

"Much more efficient," said Edgar.

"Well, I appreciate your advice," said Herb, "but just trust me. I think we have to keep the alarm system for a while—at least until the hurricane season is over."

"If you want to be stubborn and stupid," said Graham, "go right ahead. But we've warned you."

"If you want to be an outcast and a laughing-stock," said Pam, "that's your privilege, Herb."

Edgar started to say something, but suddenly he began to yawn, and he had to cover his beak with one wing. The sound of the yawn came through the feathers, slightly muffled. The three animals marched away together, without looking back.

Herb watched them for a while. He was angry, and his feelings were hurt too. He started to fix his broken picket fence. His garden was a wreck, too, but he decided: first the fence, then the garden. There'd be time for that later, unless something else happened. "Maybe I'm not a leader after all," Herb said, half aloud. "Maybe everybody thinks I'm a joke."

In the clubhouse in the woods, Clyde, the old turtle, who had slept through the false alarm, woke up and decided to go out and get some fresh air. Clyde crawled very quietly across the top of the pool table so as not to wake Arthur, who was still sound asleep in the wicker chair. But as Clyde crept down the chute inside the pool table on his way out, he dislodged a pool ball, which rumbled down the chute ahead of him, and banged into the other pool balls with a great clatter.

Arthur woke with a start. "What?" he said.

"It's nothing, Arthur," called Clyde from inside the pool table, his voice echoing. "Go back to sleep-eep-eep...."

"Where are you?" asked Arthur.

"In the pool table," said Clyde. "I'm heading home-ome-ome...."

"Goodness," said Arthur. "Home? I should be on my way home, too. I have a million things to do." He staggered to his feet. "I shouldn't even have sat down," he said, waddling to the door. "See you later, Clyde," he called, blinking into the sunlight.

"Goodbye-yi-yi-yi...." echoed Clyde's voice from the darkness.

Arthur hurried through the woods. He remembered he had had a list of things to do, but he couldn't recall just what he had done with it. He had also forgotten what was on the list. His wife might be rather upset, he realized. He wondered what to do. He had been gone for several hours, and not done one single errand or chore. "Oh, my," he murmured aloud. "Oh, my."

Walking as fast as he could along the path toward his house, Arthur noticed some sunflowers. Perhaps his wife would like a bouquet of them, he thought. They looked very nice indeed. A bunch of sunflowers just might make her feel very pleasant, especially if she had been wondering why Arthur had not come home. If she were upset about him not doing any of the things he was supposed to do, or about him losing the list, well...a large bunch of lovely sunflowers would surely make her feel better. Arthur picked a half a dozen, and continued homeward, peering over the top of the sunflowers.

As he came to the stream, he walked very cautiously, making sure not to fall in. It certainly would not do, he realized, to arrive home covered with mud. He stepped onto a

broad rock in the middle of the stream, then took a big step up onto the other bank. He felt his foot slip, so he reached out with one paw to grab a sapling for balance, and, as he did so, one of the sunflowers dropped quietly into the stream. Arthur did not notice it, however, and he hoisted himself onto the bank, and continued homeward.

The sunflower went down the stream slowly, bumping the edges as it went; catching for a second on a twig; resting briefly against a rock, then floating free again, and moving more rapidly down toward the waterfall.

As the flower floated below the big elm tree where Desmond was sitting, Desmond happened to look down, and he spotted it. His eyes popped. "I didn't do it!" he yelled. "It's not my fault! I didn't drop the sunflower!" He was still clutching his own sunflower tightly. "It's not a hurricane!" he cried, glancing at the sky to make sure. "Don't be alarmed, everybody! It's not a hurricane!"

"What's Desmond shouting?" asked one of

the chipmunks, running along the branch of a tree.

"Something about an alarm," answered a second chipmunk nervously, "and I think he said 'hurricane.'"

"Hurricane?" A bunch of sparrows dove twittering out of the trees, and flew off in all directions, shrieking about a hurricane coming. On the ground, other animals began to run around frantically, tripping over stones and roots. "Hurricane!" they cried.

Desmond decided he must stop that sunflower from floating down to Kirkham's waterfall. If he didn't stop it in time, then Kirkham would surely ring the alarm, and then the entire place would be in an uproar again. Desmond jumped to a lower branch, then made a frightening dive directly to the earth, and landed with a jarring thump. He staggered to his feet, still holding his own sunflower in his teeth, and galloped along the bank of the stream in pursuit of the other sunflower. It was rough and slippery going, and Desmond—hopping over skunk cabbages, leaping from rock to rock, dodging trees and stumps—couldn't seem to catch up. The sunflower floated along, just ahead of him. Suddenly, there was the waterfall, not ten yards away. Desmond made a fierce effort to catch the sunflower. As the flower moved lightly toward the top of the falls, Desmond lunged at it, paws outstretched —and fell, face first, into the stream. The sunflower sailed smoothly over the waterfall just ahead of his nose.

Kirkham, sitting on his mossy rock below, saw first the sunflower come over the falls, and then saw Desmond—with a second sunflower clenched in his teeth—come tumbling over the edge behind it. "Wow!" boomed Kirkham. "A *two*-sunflower alarm! This must be the *real* thing!" He leaped up and began tugging on the overhead vine. A moment later, Desmond lifted his head out of the water in the broad pool, and saw Kirkham swinging back and forth on the vine. Kirkham had a frantic look in his enormous eyes. "Don't

worry, Desmond!" called Kirkham, as he swung past Desmond's head, "I'm giving the alarm as fast as I can!"

The next thing Desmond heard was the bell, clanging furiously in the meadow.

Chapter
7

An hour later, after the second false alarm was over, Harvey and Pete went up to Herb's house to see if they could cheer up their uncle. They knew he would be feeling awful. Most of the animals were quite upset and angry at Herb for causing them to get excited about two hurricanes that didn't happen, and a lot of them weren't even speaking to Herb. They just glared at him on their way by his house.

As Harvey and Pete climbed over the stone wall they met Graham, the grumpy rabbit, coming down the hill. "Hello," said Harvey. "Hi," said Pete.

"I hope *you* boys weren't involved in this stupid and outrageous business," barked Graham.

"What stupid business?" asked Pete.

"You know very well what stupid business," said Graham. "Herb's stupid hurricane business."

"Oh," said Harvey. "*That* business."

"Of course," said Graham. "Well, it's all over now. I've just told your uncle that everybody around here wants him to pack up and get out. They've had enough of his nonsense!" Graham climbed over the wall, and strode away down the road.

Harvey and Pete looked at each other. Was it possible that Uncle Herb would leave? They ran quickly up the meadow to his house. He was nowhere in sight.

"Uncle Herb?" called Harvey and Pete. "Are you here?" There was no answer. Herb's place was a mess. The picket fence was splintered, the flowers were trampled, and the old bell was lying on its side in the tall grass.

Harvey and Pete peered in the door. Herb was sitting in his beach chair, his back to the view, staring at the wall.

"Hi, Uncle Herb," said Harvey softly. "It's us."

"Who?" asked Herb.

"Harvey and Pete."

"Oh," said Herb. He didn't move.

Harvey and Pete stood quietly for a while looking at him, not knowing what to do.

"We know it wasn't your fault," Pete said, finally.

"If there had been a storm," added Harvey, "all the animals would be very grateful to you now."

"There wasn't any storm," murmured Herb.

"That wasn't your fault," said Harvey. He thought for a moment. Then he said, "Maybe we can figure how to make the alarm system

101

work better. We could try to fix it up so that there wouldn't be any more false alarms. We could—"

Herb interrupted, as if he had not been listening. "I'm going to pack up my things," he said slowly and sadly, "and move away now. If you boys want any of this stuff—" he waved at the collection of shells and stones and seaweed and sticks lying on the shelf— "you can have it. Just help yourselves. I don't care...."

"You can't move away, Uncle Herb," said Harvey. "You're the leader around here."

"Yes," added Pete. "Everybody counts on you."

Herb shook his head. "Not anymore," he said. "They'll have to find somebody else."

Harvey and Pete didn't know what to say. They looked at Herb's collection of stuff for a few moments. Then, finally, Pete asked, "But where would you go?"

"Doesn't matter," said Herb. He slumped lower in his chair. "Just away...away from the beach, and the woods, and the meadow, and ...all the things I like." He wiped his eye with one paw. "Away from here. It doesn't matter where."

He was silent again, and Harvey and Pete knew there was nothing for them to say, so they walked quietly out of the dim house into the bright meadow.

They walked down the hill in silence, crossed the dirt road, and headed for the beach. As they climbed over the high part of the beach, where beach plums and wild cherry trees and bayberry bushes made a small forest, they saw a group of sandpipers running around on the shore below.

"Let's not go down there," said Harvey. "They're probably all saying bad things about Uncle Herb."

"OK," said Pete. "Where should we go?"

Harvey glanced around. "The marsh?" he said.

"Let's go," said Pete.

They walked down to the broad, shallow marsh. The tide was out, and the mud was glistening in the sunlight. Harvey and Pete trudged along, their feet making splendid

glooping noises in the squishy mud. "I wish we could help Uncle Herb," said Harvey. "He's the best rabbit in the world."

"So do I," said Pete. "But how?"

"I don't know," said Harvey. "It's really sad."

"Boys! Yoo hoo! *Boys!*" A sharp, shrill voice cut through the air. Harvey and Pete turned, and saw Loretta, the old blue heron, stalking toward them. Her eyes glittered, and feathers stuck out from her head.

"Good morning, ma'am," said Harvey and Pete.

"*Must* you come traipsing through here, making a racket?" she demanded. "If you want to crash around, why don't you do it in the woods where it won't bother anybody? We like to keep the marsh very quiet. Do you under-stand?"

"I understand," said Harvey.

"So do I," said Pete.

"It's been a thoroughly unpleasant day," continued Loretta. "Animals running around and screaming about hurricanes. That's what

happens when rabbits start thinking that they're important—"

"We'll be hurrying along now," said Harvey.

"I don't mean to be cross," shrieked Loretta, as Harvey and Pete moved rapidly away, "but we do like people to behave themselves around here! We can't permit exceptions!"

Harvey and Pete climbed up onto one of the grassy islands where the footing was better, and they began to run. They raced along until Loretta was only a small dot in the distance. Then they stopped for breath, and sat down.

"Hi, guys," said a voice.

They looked down and saw Larry, the fiddler crab, coming out of a hole in the steep side of the island. "Hi, Larry," said Harvey and Pete.

"Had a run-in with the old bag, huh?" said Larry. "I could hear her from inside."

"She told us to be quiet," said Pete.

"Yeah, well," said Larry. "She's a real bird, you know what I mean? I'd like to give her a quick shot with the old claw—" Larry opened and closed his pincher—"but I can never get close enough. How's tricks?"

"Not too good," said Harvey, glumly.

"What's happening around here?" asked Pete, trying to change the subject.

"Oh, well, you know," said Larry. "The tide comes in, the tide goes out. That's the main action." He shrugged his claw.

"Pretty dull, huh?" said Harvey.

"Oh, you get used to it," said Larry. "You pace yourself. You don't get too worked up, or expect too much. You know what I mean? Then when the tide comes in, you say, 'Hey— the tide's coming in!' and you try to enjoy that. But by and large, yeah, it's a drag."

"Do you ever go anywhere?" asked Pete.

"Nah, not much," said Larry. "Oh, I once went up the river—" he pointed with his claw toward the end of the marsh— "and that was nice. But it took me about a year. I'm mostly hanging around here now. It's not so bad." He looked at Harvey and Pete closely. "Say, you guys look down in the dumps. What's the matter?"

"Oh, Uncle Herb is in trouble," said

Harvey. He told Larry about the false alarms, and how everybody was mad at Herb now.

"That's a shame," said Larry. "Old Herb was just trying to help everybody, and now he's in disgrace, huh?"

"What can we do to help him, Larry?" asked Pete. "You got any ideas?"

"*Me?*" said Larry. "I don't have ideas. I haven't had an idea in as long as I can remember. You know me. I just watch the tide come in, the tide go out...." Larry shrugged. "I'm sorry. Why don't you ask Dunlop the beaver? He's got ideas."

"Dunlop?" said Pete.

"Dunlop!" cried Harvey. "Of course."

"Dunlop would know what to do!" said Pete.

"That was a good idea, Larry," said Harvey.

Larry seemed to be blushing. "Really?" he said. "A good idea? Thank you. It's my first, you know."

"It's a good start," said Harvey. "Come on, Pete, let's go find Dunlop."

Larry watched them, as they went across the marsh toward the river. They turned and waved, and Larry raised his claw in farewell. "My first idea," he said to himself, "and a good one. How 'bout that?" He looked around. "Maybe I'll have another one sometime. Who knows?"

It took Harvey and Pete about twenty minutes to reach Dunlop's place. A lot of fallen trees and branches and reeds were piled along the bank of the river. Dunlop wasn't around, so Harvey and Pete looked at the dams Dunlop had built in the middle of the river. "He must be an excellent beaver," said Harvey. "Those dams look very well built."

"Yeah, but he can be very cross, too," said Pete. "We better watch out."

There was a loud splash. "What do *you* want?" demanded Dunlop, coming up out of the water abruptly a few feet away, and glaring at Harvey and Pete. His fur was soaked and matted.

"Hi," said Harvey. "We just came to say hello."

110

"Hello," said Pete. They both smiled at Dunlop hopefully.

"That's it?" demanded Dunlop. "Just came to say hello?"

They nodded.

"Well, hello and goodbye," said Dunlop.

"Well, we were thinking maybe we could look around," said Harvey. Pete nodded.

"Why don't you go someplace else and look around?" Dunlop growled, standing in his own puddle, dripping.

"Well, it's more interesting here. You've got more stuff lying around, and more things are happening."

Dunlop stared at Harvey. Then he grunted, picked up a stick, examined it, and threw it toward a pile of wood. "Oh," he said finally, "you can hang around for a while, I guess. But don't touch anything! Don't mess around! I've got everything exactly where I want it."

"You do?" said Harvey, looking at all the fallen trees and scattered branches, and half-chewed logs, and heaps of wood chips, and piles of rocks, leaves, weeds, and cattails lying on the bank of the river.

"Darn right!" said Dunlop, kicking a stone.

Neither Pete nor Harvey knew what to say to that, so finally Harvey asked politely, "What are you doing these days, Mr. Dunlop?"

"What am I *doing*?" roared Dunlop. His eyes bulged, and he smacked his large, flat tail on the ground. Harvey and Pete stepped back.

"Oh, I'm doing a few little things," Dunlop said, in a somewhat lower voice, "such as... climbing up those steep hills back there, climbing for a mile or two through tangles and brambles that no one has ever been able to get through except me, and then searching for hours for the perfect trees, and then cutting them down cleanly and neatly with my own personal teeth in about two minutes flat, and then getting out of the way very briskly since I know precisely which way they are going to fall, and then—crash! crash! crash!—down they come, and then I drag those trees personally with my own unbelievable strength for a mile or two down through those same tangles and brambles to the river bank here, where, after the shortest of breathers, I pitch right in again and proceed to build astonishing dams and fantastic homes and unbelievable waterways— each and every one an undertaking of the most complex and difficult sort, requiring enormous physical strength, vast dedication, plenty of technical know-how, and a lot of old-fashioned pizzazz—which when finished, and I am referring to those dams, homes, and waterways, will last for years and years and years beyond anything else anybody else around here is doing!" He glared at them. *That's* what I'm doing," he said, and sat down.

"Oh," said Harvey.

"You certainly are busy," said Pete.

"Darn right I'm busy!" exclaimed Dunlop. "I'm busy as a beaver. Didn't you ever hear that?"

"How come you work so hard?" asked Pete.

"It beats me," said Dunlop, gazing out at the river with all the dams and houses jutting up this way and that.

"Do you like building all these things?" asked Harvey.

"I like it, and I hate it," said Dunlop. "On the one hand, it's the greatest work ever done by animal—"

"Must be," said Pete.

"—And it's a real drag, too," said Dunlop. "Beyond that, I haven't reached any big conclusion."

Harvey waited to make sure that Dunlop

wasn't about to say anything more, and then he asked, "We were wondering if you could help us with something."

"What?" said Dunlop.

"We need some ideas and advice," said Harvey.

"Why didn't you ask one of those dumb animals out where you live to help you?" demanded Dunlop.

"We need somebody that's really smart," said Pete.

"None of them is anywhere near smart enough," added Harvey.

"Oh, I see," said Dunlop, nodding. "It's *wisdom* you're after."

"Yes," said Harvey.

"Right," said Pete.

"What seems to be the problem?" asked Dunlop, pleasantly.

Five minutes later, Harvey and Pete had told the whole story. Dunlop chewed on a willow branch while he listened. "I see," he said, at the end. "Your Uncle Herb is in trouble because he got everybody stirred up and scared and running around, and then there wasn't any hurricane. Correct?"

The boys nodded.

Dunlop stood up. "I've heard of worse problems," he said. He threw the willow branch in the river, and watched it float away.

"What do you think?" asked Pete. "Have you got any ideas?"

"Do you?" asked Harvey.

"Of course I have ideas," snapped Dunlop abruptly. "Just stop yapping at me." He smacked his tail on the mud.

"Sorry," said Harvey and Pete.

Dunlop walked up and down the shore for a few moments, then said, "Do you have any friends?"

"Friends?" asked Harvey.

"What kind?" asked Pete.

"The kind that would help you when you're in a pinch," said Dunlop. "You got any of those?"

"Well, there's a lot of kids our age," said Harvey. "There's Phil and Franny, the chipmunks, and Murray and Henry and Horace, the birds—there's Shirley, the raccoon, and her little brother, Kenneth—"

"There's Fred and Eileen and Lew, the squirrels," said Pete. "And Donald and Barbara and—"

"All right!" cried Dunlop. "But tell me this: Are any of them any good?"

"Good?" asked Harvey.

"Have they got any gumption?" yelled Dunlop. "Have they got any snap, any fight?" Dunlop climbed onto a tree stump. "Are they wishy-washy, or will they do the job? Are they whiners, or winners, or what?"

"A little of each," said Harvey. "I guess."

"Will they let you down when the going gets rough?" cried Dunlop.

"Never!" yelled Pete. "Never!"

"How do *you* know?" whispered Harvey.

"I don't," whispered Pete. "It just seemed the thing to say." He shrugged.

Dunlop wasn't really listening anyway. He was waving his paws, and jumping around on the stump, and roaring, "Will they follow you through thick and thin? Rough and smooth? Rain or shine?"

"Yes!" cried Pete.

"Have they got any guts?" yelled Dunlop. "Or do they give you excuses? What do you say?"

"Yes, about the guts," cried Harvey. "No, about the excuses."

"Are they first-rate, top-drawer, loyal and trusty and true?" demanded Dunlop.

"Always!" yelled Pete.

"Have they got what it takes?" shouted Dunlop. "Will they take what they get? Will they get what they go for?"

"Yes! Yes! *Yes!*" yelled Harvey and Pete.

"Then follow me!" cried Dunlop. He jumped off the stump, strode away down the river bank, and Harvey and Pete ran after him.

Chapter
8

The sun was going down over the rocky islands, the sea was smooth and pink and still, and, in the yard under the big maple tree, Rudy and Blanche Kipney's party was going strong. The guests—owls, raccoons, turtles, woodchucks, squirrels, frogs, birds, rabbits, and many smaller animals—stood laughing and chatting and eating rolled-up skunk-cabbage leaves with mushroom-acorn dip. (Almost everybody from the meadow and the woods and the beach and the marsh was there, except for Cyrus, Desmond, Kirkham, and Herb, who knew that they would not be welcome.) Even Stanley the snake was there, curled up on the table next to the mushroom-acorn dip, talking to everybody. During both hurricane false alarms, Stanley had slithered into the Kipneys'

yard, asking for shelter in their maple tree. And the second time he turned up, Blanche felt she had to invite him to the party. ("Party?" Stanley had said, acting very surprised. "Party? Why, I might be able to come.")

Graham, the big gray rabbit, was leaning against the maple tree, making a little speech to several of the guests. "Now, I happen to know a good deal about weather and storms," he was saying, "and that's why I didn't pay any attention at all to what Herb said today. I *knew* there wouldn't be any storm."

"You're a lot smarter than *some* rabbits we know," said Pam the skunk.

"Thank you," chuckled Graham. "But don't be too hard on old Herb," he added, smiling generously. "He doesn't mean any harm, and as long as we don't listen to what he says, we'll be all right." He chuckled again, and everybody laughed with him.

"*You're* the leader around here," said Edgar the owl.

"That's right," said several animals.

"Say, Graham," piped a tiny voice from down by Graham's foot, "when are we going to have another game of Acorn?"

Graham glanced down and saw Earl the snail. "When I can find the time, Earl," said Graham irritably. Then he turned back to his admiring listeners. "As I was saying," he continued, "I knew there wouldn't be a storm today, so I didn't get excited or panic when that bell rang. I kept a calm, level head."

"Tell us, Graham," said Loretta, the blue heron, "aren't there warning signs before a big storm? That's what I've always heard."

"Absolutely, Loretta," said Graham. "Everybody knows that—except maybe Herb." Everybody laughed again.

"Tell us, Graham," said Pam. "What are the signs?"

"Well," began Graham, clearing his throat and taking a deep breath, "one of the very first signs is the movement of air—or to put it in simple terms: wind." He looked around to make sure everybody understood. "You cannot have a storm without wind." Everybody nodded.

At that moment, far away in the meadow, a bell—Herb's bell—began to ring.

"There goes that silly bell again," said Pam.

"Oh for goodness sakes," said Loretta.

"Ignore it," said Edgar.

"Go on now, Graham," said Loretta earnestly. "We're all listening."

Graham took another deep breath. "The wind is usually noticeable in two ways, which I will call *A* and *B*. You should all learn to recognize these ways. *A* is what you observe with your eyes: namely, trees bending and shaking, grass waving, et cetera. Everybody understand so far?"

The animals nodded solemnly.

"We will then move on to method *B*," declared Graham. "Method *B* refers to the sound of wind, which you hear with your *ears*. This may take the form of whistling, whooshing,

wailing, or other noises. That's the only warning system anybody needs. There'll be plenty
of time to take shelter." Graham looked
around. "Any questions?" he inquired.

"If I understand this correctly," said Edgar,
"then when it is very quiet and still, there is
little chance of a storm?"

"That is right, Edgar," said Graham.
"There could not be a storm tonight, because
nothing is moving. Observe, for example, the
maple tree here—" He pointed directly overhead, and everybody looked up. "Not the
slightest bit of breeze," declared Graham,
pointing with his paw.

"It looks like a breeze to *me*," said Earl the
snail.

Graham's paw dropped, and his eyes grew
large. Just above his head, the maple tree's
leaves were shaking. In fact, the whole tree
was trembling.

"Goodness gracious!" shrieked Loretta.
"Will you look at that!" Several leaves fluttered
down, and there was a high-pitched wailing

sound from near the top of the tree. The lower branches began to wave and jiggle.

"It's the storm!" cried Blanche Kipney.

"Maybe a hurricane!" screamed Loretta.

"I observe it with methods *A* and *B*," yelled Edgar, dropping a skunk-cabbage leaf.

The wailing grew louder and louder. Acorns and twigs and leaves sailed through the air.

"Everybody take shelter!" yelled Rudy. "Hurry! Hurry! There's no time to waste!"

The guests began to run. Birds zoomed crazily in and out, as if hurled by the wind. The animals rushed past Graham, heading for the road. "Wait!" shouted Graham. "There isn't even any *rain*!" No sooner had he spoken than Graham was struck with a huge sheet of water, then another. He was soaked. Graham wiped his face, and shrieked, "It's the real thing, all right! Everybody run!" Another shower of water hit him with a loud splat. "This is going to be a *big* one!" he cried, and ran for the road, holding both paws over his head.

In an instant, the Kipneys had dashed into

their house in the tree, and slammed the door. The other guests were hurrying down the road, heading for their homes and shelters. Only Stanley the snake was left behind. He slithered down the leg of the table, crossed the clearing, and disappeared under a large rock.

Down the road, Graham caught up with Edgar and Pam, and passed them. "Wait for us!" they yelled.

"Hurry up!" replied Graham. A hailstorm of acorns struck him as he ran, then a shower of cold water caught him on the back of the neck. He came skidding around the corner of the road where the path to his house began, and he dashed down the path. A tall tree suddenly came crashing down directly in front of him. Terrified, Graham climbed over it as fast as he could, and raced to his front door. He jumped inside, and slammed the door behind him.

A few moments later, Edgar and Pam were pounding on the door. "Let us in, you old fool!" shrieked Pam. "This is a hurricane!"

Graham opened the door just wide enough

to let them in, then bolted it behind them. "We should have listened to Herb in the first place," snapped Edgar, shaking his wet feathers and spraying water all over Graham.

"You said it, Edgar," agreed Pam. "Graham doesn't know a sunset from a snowstorm."

"I don't understand this at all," grumbled Graham, wiping himself with a towel. He went to the window and tried to see out. It was hard, because rain was splashing against the window, and a large branch was slapping back and forth against the glass, and a stream of acorns, sticks, and grasses was flying by. There was a steady pounding on the roof, as if hailstones were falling. Graham began trembling. "I just hope I live through this hurricane," he whimpered, and crawled under his dining-room table to hide.

"Make room for me, stupid!" screeched Edgar.

"Me, too!" cried Pam, and all three crowded in under the table, as the noise outside grew worse.

Up on top of Graham's roof, out of sight,

Harvey and Pete were jumping up and down, making a terrible din. "Keep it up, Pete!" whispered Harvey. "Faster!" At the edge of the roof, Phil and Franny, the chipmunks, were pouring buckets of water over the side so that it went right past the window below. Eileen and Lew, the squirrels, were kicking heaps of leaves and twigs and acorns off the roof, and Kenneth the raccoon was swinging a big branch against the window. Several birds flew past the window again and again.

"This must look like a very scary hurricane to Graham," said Pete.

"Look," said Harvey, pointing into the woods a few yards away. "Dunlop is going to chop down another tree!"

Dunlop waved to them from the bushes, and chewed through the last few inches of a tall hemlock tree. Then he gave it a shove, and, with a terrible splintering noise, the entire tree toppled over and crashed directly in front of Graham's window, shaking the whole house.

"How are you guys doing?" asked Desmond

the squirrel, dropping onto the roof from an overhanging branch. "You need any help?"

"We're OK," said Harvey. "Did everybody run away from the Kipneys' party?"

"They sure did," said Desmond. "We soaked old Graham about three times, and shook up the trees, and jumped up and down on the branches, and dropped a lot of acorns, and everybody took off like a shot. The place is deserted."

The bell in the meadow was still ringing. "That's Cyrus the sea gull," said Harvey. "He's flying around with it, giving the alarm."

"Where's all the rest of the kids?" asked Desmond.

"Dunlop assigned them to make sure all the grown-ups stayed in their houses. If any grown-ups stick their heads out, the children are going to throw acorns and water and stuff so that the grown-ups will think the storm is still going on."

Desmond nodded. "Dunlop certainly figured out what to do, didn't he?" he said. "He's one smart beaver."

"Thank you," said Dunlop, climbing up onto the roof. He stood up and looked around. "I think we can ease up a bit," he said. "It's getting dark, and I believe most of the animals will stay in their homes for the night now."

"OK," said Harvey.

"Right," said Pete.

"By tomorrow morning," said Dunlop, "everybody will consider Herb a hero."

"That's great," said Harvey.

"Thanks for your help," Pete said.

"Never mind *that*," said Dunlop. "You all performed admirably. The job is done. We have triumphed, and I am going home." He jumped off the back of the roof, and started to walk away. "Goodbye," he called, and then he was out of sight.

"Goodbye," called Harvey and Pete and Desmond.

There was only the sound of snapping twigs, and then it was quiet. Dunlop was gone.

Deep in the woods, at that very moment, Herb was sleeping. He had not heard the distant bell, or the shouting of the animals, or any sounds at all, except the noises of the stream where it gurgled over some rocks and sunken logs. Herb had left his house in the meadow late in the afternoon, had walked out with a few possessions, and closed the door, and then wandered into the woods. He hadn't said good-bye to anybody at all. His only plan was to keep on walking, until he found a new place to live —a place far away from the animals he knew. But he had grown tired as he walked through the woods, getting farther and farther away from his old home, and as darkness came down —early, as it does in the woods—Herb no longer had the strength to go on. There was a stream ahead, and Herb went toward it, not knowing whether it was the same one that went by Kirkham's waterfall or not; not caring. He was just tired. He reached the stream, and sat down on the mossy bank. He listened to the sounds of it, and soon his eyes began to close. He pushed some old leaves into a pile, then stretched out, and used the pile for a pillow.

The leaves crunched under his head, the stream gulped and rippled by, and Herb was soon asleep, dreaming lonely dreams about places and friends he would never see again.

Chapter
9

It began in the very early hours of the morning, when almost everybody was asleep. (Even Edgar, who was usually up and about during the nighttime, was snoring in his tree top, worn out from the excitement of the evening. When Dunlop's storm had let up a bit at Graham's house, Edgar had crept out from under the table, opened the door, and flapped directly home to his tree. Almost immediately, he had gone to sleep.)

There was nobody around to notice, or to give the alarm.

Nobody saw the waves growing bigger and bigger. Nobody saw the whitecaps, or heard the booming thunder of the surf. Nobody noticed the wind rising, whistling through the woods.

By the time the animals were roused from

their sleep by the crashing of the trees and the roar of the wind, there was nothing for them to do about it except to huddle down in their houses and burrows and nests, and hope that the hurricane—for that is what it was: a hurricane; a real one, whirling in from the sea, tearing through the woods and fields—would go away. Graham opened the front door of his house a crack to take a peek, and the wind ripped the door from its hinges, flung it bounding across the road and into the sky. Graham watched in horror, then dived under his table again.

Edgar finally woke up and felt his whole tree swaying back and forth in the wind. He felt seasick, and he was sure that at any moment the tree would snap. "Why didn't I listen to Herb?" he screeched.

For two hours, the storm spun through the meadows and the marsh and the woods; grabbing whatever it could and throwing it into the the dark sky, breaking what could be broken, moving whatever could be moved.

And then it was over. The waves subsided, and the wind disappeared, and the air was soft and warm. The sun came up, and the pink sky turned to blue, with no clouds in sight at all.

Harvey and Pete went exploring as soon as it was light. They raced through broad, deep puddles in the road, kicking and splashing. They ran to the beach, and found that everything was changed. "Look at all the new logs and trees!" yelled Harvey.

"Let's climb 'em!" cried Pete.

They quickly ran up and down the tree trunks, balancing on the branches, then jumping down onto the smooth sand. "Look at the seaweed!" yelled Pete. Mountains of kelp were shining in the sun, and the boys poked through the slippery piles in search of treasure. Then they raced up to the woods, and climbed more trees; broken branches hung down to the ground, and Harvey and Pete used them as ladders to reach places they had never been before. They sat in the highest branches of trees they had never dreamed of climbing, and they looked out over the changed land.

"This is the best day *I've* ever seen," said Harvey.

"Same here," said Pete.

Through the branches, they could see the roof of Herb's house in the meadow, and the trampled garden, and, scattered across the field, bits of Herb's picket fence. Harvey and Pete gazed at the deserted-looking house.

"Where do you think he went?" asked Pete.

"I don't know," said Harvey.

"I wish he'd come back," said Pete.

Several hours earlier, as the hurricane roared through the deep woods, Herb, lying at the edge of the stream, had been hit by what seemed to be a large rock. It struck him just behind the ear, and he sat up with a cry. "Ow!" he yelled.

"Sorry," came a small, old voice from the darkness.

"Who said that?" demanded Herb.

"Me," said the voice.

"Who's 'me'?" said Herb.

"Clyde," said the voice.

"*Clyde*?" repeated Herb. "My turtle friend from back home?"

"Yes," said Clyde irritably. "This darn hurricane has been banging me around all over the place."

"*Hurricane*?" said Herb.

"You bet!" said Clyde. "It's a real lollapalooza."

"What about Harvey and Pete and the others?" Herb cried.

"Who knows," said Clyde.

"I've got to go help them!" said Herb. He tried to get up, but the wind knocked him flat.

"No use trying to get anywhere in *this* hurricane," said Clyde. "Would you mind putting a rock or something on top of my shell? I'm sick of being thrown around by this wind."

Herb found a large rock in the darkness at the edge of the stream, and put it carefully on top of Clyde's shell. "There," Herb said. "That ought to keep you in one place for a while."

The wind wailed through the trees overhead, and the branches thrashed about. Herb sat hunched against the tree, worrying about the animals back home, and waiting for the storm to die down.

Harvey and Pete were climbing down from the highest tree of all, when they suddenly saw

Herb coming out of the woods below them. He was giving Clyde a ride, holding the old turtle under one arm like a football.

"Uncle Herb!" they yelled. "Welcome back!"

"Hello, Harvey! Hello, Pete!" called Herb. "Are you all right? Is everybody OK?"

"Everybody's fine!" they yelled. Harvey and Pete ran to greet Herb. "Where were you, Uncle Herb?" asked Harvey, when they reached him.

"Oh, nowhere to speak of," said Herb. "The main thing is, I'm back, and it's time to get busy." He glanced around. "That hurricane made a mess, didn't it?" He rubbed his paws together. "Got to get things organized...." He looked very happy.

"Well, thanks for the lift, Herb," said Clyde. "I think I'll walk the rest of the way." Herb put Clyde down in the meadow.

"It's Herb!" yelled Desmond, from a tree top. "Herb's back!" In an instant, the cry was being passed across the meadow and through the woods. From the beach and the marsh came the sound of voices saying, "Herb's back! Herb!"

Herb strolled across the field to his house, with Harvey and Pete at his side. By the time Herb reached his old garden, Graham, Pam, and Edgar were standing together, waiting for him. Cyrus came in for a landing on the roof, and a lot of other animals began arriving from the woods. Herb greeted them all, and asked, "What's going on?"

Graham looked rather embarrassed. "Well, Herb," he began, "first of all, a lot of us want to say we're sorry that we didn't believe you when you said there was going to be a hurricane—"

"And we want to thank you for warning us," cut in Edgar. "Arthur and Cyrus told us those false alarms weren't your fault."

"You saved our lives with your warning system!" added Pam.

All the other animals clapped. Herb gave a small bow, waved to everybody, and smiled. He was feeling very pleased. Then he bent

down and whispered in Harvey's ear, "Do you think they expect me to give a speech?"

Harvey thought for a second. "No, I don't think so."

"Not even a very short speech?" whispered Herb.

"You don't have to," said Harvey.

"I don't really mind," whispered Herb. "If that's what they want."

"They don't seem to expect a speech," said Harvey.

"Well, it's probably the thing to do," said Herb. "I don't want to disappoint them." He stood up straight, trying to get his thoughts in order. It should be a short speech, he thought, but inspiring. And he shouldn't fail to mention the names of some of the animals who helped—

"Herb?" called a voice. It was Loretta the heron. "There's a great deal of work to be done around here, getting everything fixed up. You're the leader. Will you be in charge?"

Herb nodded. "Why, yes," he replied. "I'll

be in charge." All the animals clapped and cheered.

"Let's get started!" cried Graham, and suddenly all the animals were hurrying away across the meadow, going to their homes to begin work. Herb was left alone with Harvey and Pete. It was quite silent. Herb looked around.

"Well," he said, "I guess I don't have to give a speech after all...." He walked to the front door of his house, and peered inside. "Doesn't look too bad," he said. He went in, then came out a moment later, hauling his old beach chair. He set it up in the garden, facing out over the meadow and the beach and the sea.

"We'll gather up the pieces of the fence, Uncle Herb," said Harvey. "Is that OK?"

"First-rate, excellent, and splendid," said Herb. The two young rabbits ran into the field, and Herb sank slowly into the beach chair. The sun was very warm, and there was just the right amount of breeze. Herb gazed at the sky, the tree tops, the meadow full of wildflowers, and the marsh, the beach, and the blue sea stretching smoothly on and on and on, and then he murmured to himself, "This is probably ... the most perfect day ... I've ever seen ... in my entire life."